The Little Puppy

A Random House PICTUREBACK®

The Little Puppy

Story by **Judy Dunn**

Photographs by **Phoebe Dunn**

Random House 🏠 New York

Text copyright © 1984 by Judy Dunn Spangenberg. Photographs copyright © 1984 by Phoebe Dunn. All rights reserved under International and Pan-American Copyright Conventions. Published in the United States by Random House, Inc., New York, and simultaneously in Canada by Random House of Canada Limited, Toronto.

Library of Congress Cataloging in Publication Data: Dunn, Judy. The little puppy. SUMMARY: A boy and his dog enjoy their first months together. 1. Dogs—Juvenile fiction [1. Dogs—Fiction] I. Dunn, Phoebe, ill. II. Title. PZ10.3.D8815Li 1984 [E] 84-2031 ISBN: 0-394-86595-2 (pbk.); 0-394-96595-7 (lib. bdg.)

Manufactured in the United States of America   48 47 46 45 44

Tim felt lonely. Summer vacation was starting and there was no one nearby for him to play with.

Then one day, early in the summer, Tim heard some exciting news. The next-door neighbor's dog had just had six puppies. Tim had always wanted a dog.

Every day Tim went next door to see the puppies. He begged his parents to let him have one. Finally they agreed.

Tim could hardly wait to bring his puppy home. But the puppies were still too small to leave their mother.

Tim and his father built a bed for the puppy. They measured and sawed and hammered until it was perfect.

"A puppy is a lot of work, Tim," said his father. "You will have to take care of it every day."

Tim promised that he would. Then he painted the puppy's box all by himself.

At last the puppies were old enough to leave their mother. Tim went next door to pick one out. He played with each puppy and tried to choose his favorite. But it was hard. All the puppies were wiggly and warm and friendly.

"Maybe I'll take *you* home,"
Tim said to one puppy.

"Or maybe you," he said to
another. He just couldn't decide
which one he wanted.

But Tim never did get to choose a puppy —because one little puppy chose him! The puppy stretched up to lick Tim's chin. Tim picked him up gently. The puppy wagged his stubby tail.

"Now, what will I name you?" wondered Tim. He thought hard. Finally he said, "You look like Charlie to me."

Tim carried Charlie to his new home.

Charlie was lonely the first night in his new bed. He missed his brothers and sisters. Tim put a ticking alarm clock in the bed to keep Charlie company, but the puppy still whined and howled.

Charlie saw Tim's toy dog lying on the floor. It was just what the lonely puppy needed. He jumped out of bed and dragged the toy into his box. Then he flopped down on its soft back and was soon fast asleep.

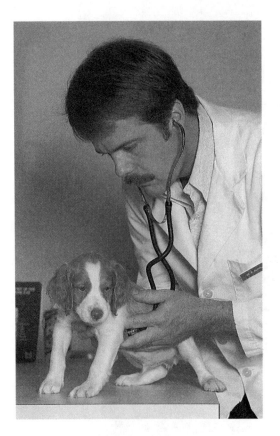

The next day Tim took Charlie to see the vet. Dr. McFarland listened to the puppy's heart and gave him a shot to keep him healthy.

Charlie didn't bark or cry once. "Good dog," said Tim, and he patted his brave puppy.

Charlie soon got used to his new home. He liked to explore all the new things.

Tim and Charlie were usually together all day. But once Tim left Charlie alone on the porch. That was a mistake.

Charlie sniffed some flowers in a pot and—whoops!—what a mess!

Then the little puppy jumped up on a chair with his dirty feet. When Tim found him, he gave Charlie a big scolding.

Tim and Charlie had lots of fun together. Charlie's favorite toy was a squishy red ball. Tim would roll it across the lawn, and Charlie would chase it as fast as he could.

Charlie would grab the ball with his teeth and carry it back to Tim. Then the game would begin again. Sometimes, though, Charlie forgot to let go of the ball!

Near the end of the summer Tim visited his
grandfather at the lake. Of course, Charlie went with
him. They both liked to sit on the dock in the warm sun.

Charlie wasn't allowed to go in the rowboat with Grandpa and Tim.

"You don't know how to swim," Tim said. "You can come with us next summer."

But Charlie couldn't wait that long. SPLASH! He paddled after the boat.

Grandpa pulled Charlie out of the water. The little puppy was wet and shivering. Grandpa dried him off and wrapped him in a soft towel to keep him warm. The puppy was all tired out.

The next day Charlie went along in the rowboat.

"He sure fooled us!" Tim said. "He doesn't need any swimming lessons."

Autumn came and Tim went back to school. Charlie didn't understand why his friend left him every day. The first day he howled.

But Charlie learned to wait patiently on the porch for Tim. As soon as he saw Tim walking up the street, he raced to meet him.

Every afternoon Tim romped with Charlie before doing his homework. The pup was big enough to play football now. He loved to grab the ball from Tim and run away with it.

Touchdown for Charlie!

When Tim had to rake leaves, Charlie
thought it was a new game.

"Hey, cut it out, Charlie!" Tim laughed.

Now Charlie was big enough to go on long walks with Tim. One sunny weekend they went exploring in the woods.

The woods were full of the scents of animals. Charlie wanted to follow them. Tim took off his leash.

Charlie sniffed along the ground
and into holes. One scent led him to
a raccoon! Charlie barked wildly and
chased it up a tree.

Tim and Charlie did everything together. "You're my best friend, Charlie," said Tim. "We'll be friends forever."

Charlie looked at Tim and wagged his tail.